Surviving The Sins

Answering the Call

By
C. A. King

Cover Design: SelfPubBookCovers.com/Ravenborn

Dedication And Acknowledgement Page

This book is dedicated to readers everywhere. Without you,
my novels would be nothing more than words on a blank page
-and-
To all participants of
NaNoWriMo
for their support and motivation throughout the years
-and-
To the elephant, otter and other critter pictures
that brighten our days and make us call for mattresses
to support the 'Thud'.

Look for other Books by C.A. King including:
The Portal Prophecies:
Book I - A Keeper's Destiny
Book II - A Halloween's Curse
Book III – Frost Bitten
Book IV - Sleeping Sands
Book V – Deadly Perceptions
Book VI – Finding Balance

Tomoiya's Story:
Book 1 – Escape to Darkness

Copyright

Cover Design: SelfPubBookCovers.com/Ravenborn

First Printing: 2016

ISBN: 978-1-988301-10-5

Kings Toe Publishing
kingstoepublishing@gmail.com
Burlington, Ontario. Canada

Prologue

Balance - the simple mention of the word invokes an image of a person walking on a tightrope, high above the ground with no net. Each footstep is carefully placed - outstretched arms teetering up and down - back and forth. Falling is not an option. In a performance, the rope is a short distance - in life, it never ends. It is that balance that keeps existence possible. To fall on either side could be deadly. One quivering footstep steadied can cause the next to wobble. Cause and effect is a concept that should be considered carefully by everyone. Unfortunately, it rarely is.

The Portal Prophecies may have saved the realms from Cornelius and Cornost, but by doing so they opened doors to new problems at the same time. One could say the rope itself is moving - not tumbling has become harder than it ever was before.

Change is inevitable in the universe. A plant that sprouts from the ground as a tiny shoot grows into a blooming flower and then withers away to seed - bringing new sprouts in the future. Some will grow in the same spot, while others will be whisked away by the wind to bring new scenery to land far away.

So too the camp changed. The guardians were free to choose their own paths: some returned to their homeworld to help rebuild and others remained in the main world to forge new futures - choosing new keepers or to have none. The new symbiotic relationship between the two came with its own problems. Something was lacking - perhaps the synergy, or trust that had been seen in the past.

The camp itself split. One group headed home with the guardians. The Shinning brothers, Jessie, Dezi and Pete, set out on a quest of their own to find a way to save their sister, Victoria, from the premature ageing that saving the lives of her family and friends caused her. Jade and Malarchy continued to forge a life in the political scene of the magical cities of the main world. Those who remained in the camp swore oaths to continue to defend the portals.

The forces that be searched for a new hero - one was chosen.

Chapter One

The contents of the bowl flew up in the air accompanied by a few shrill screams - a shower of popcorn fell back down, landing everywhere.

"Jerk!" Sarah yelled. The movie hadn't even started yet and the girls were already jumpy. "Blah." Her tongue wiggled, sticking out between her lips.

Nathan's tongue answered back, mocking her as it darted out of his mouth. He'd be back. An evening of all girls watching a horror movie was too good an opportunity to miss out on. He had every intention of making them squeal like piglets a few more times.

Shelby landed on Jade's shoulder. "I love popcorn," the avian guardian said, picking a piece out of her long blond hair before flying off again.

"Are you sure you girls are going to be alright?" William asked, delivering another bowl of popcorn.

"We'll be fine," Willow answered. "Besides, it's not like you guys aren't close by."

"If you need me, make sure you scream my name, or else I might assume you girls are just fraidy-cats and the movie scared you," William teased. With a few slight adjustments, the screen and projector were ready to go. "Just press this button when it's dark enough. The movie you ladies chose is already selected to play. I can still take everything inside if you change your minds. It could get a bit chilly out here."

"We have blankets to snuggle in," Willow said.

"And hide in," Krissy added.

A chorus of high-pitched giggles overtook the conversation. This was their night to unwind and relax together for what could be the last time.

"If you need any help with Lance," Willow started.

"We'll be fine," William interrupted. "A little male bonding time is good for a dad and his son. I got this."

"I don't know which is more frightening," Willow chuckled, watching her husband walk away. "Those two being left alone, or the movie Sarah chose."

"Hey!" Sarah yelled. "This is a hot new release. I think you'll appreciate how scary they made it. The reviews say it'll linger in your mind and haunt your dreams. I bought a new nightlight just for the occasion."

"Hey, Willow," Jessica said. "Can you make the grass softer?"

"Softer?" She asked. Her nose crinkled as one eyebrow arched up. The palms of her hands smoothed across the surface of the blanket the girls were sitting on. "Hum. I see what you mean. The tips come through the wool."

"We could put down another layer," Jade suggested.

"I asked it to be a bit more gentle," Willow offered. "I'm not sure what grass can do in this case, though." She laughed.

"Just get over it," Krissy said. Positioning herself flat on her stomach, she rested her head in her hands, propped up by her bent elbows. "It's getting dark."

"Shh," Sarah said, placing her finger in front of her mouth. Her friends had spread out all around her. She tiptoed through empty spots, attempting not to step on anyone.

"Ouch," Jessica hissed. "That hurt."

"Sorry," Sarah said. "I'm going to start the movie now. Make room for me to come back so I don't step on you again."

"Nice," Jessica muttered, rolling her eyes.

Jade snaked her arm through Willow's. "You ready for this?"

"After last year, how scary can it be?" Willow asked, chuckling.

"Shh," Sarah hissed again. "It's starting. We don't want to miss anything important."

"There's important stuff in horror flicks?" Krissy asked, squirming under a blanket to find the most comfortable position. "I thought it was all slash and gush - with blood spurting everywhere."

The journalist received a chorus of *yuck* for her remarks.

"Seems too nice out for anything to be terrifying," Jade commented.

"It's a full moon tonight," Jessica teased. "All things weird and horrible happen when the moon is full. We could be attacked by rabid werewolves." She shivered at her own words. Surveying her surroundings, she sensed an unusual calm in the air.

"It's blue," Krissy said. All eyes turned towards the sky. "You know what they say. *The really bad things happen only once in a blue moon.*"

A cool breeze rustled the leaves of nearby trees. A shadow fell over the blankets. The girls side-eyed each other. There wasn't a cloud in the sky - it was completely clear. Willow moved one hand directly into the shadow. A blue tinge coloured her skin.

"Okay," Jade cried from under a trembling blanket. "Enough with the freaky freak. Let's just watch the movie."

*****

Ring. Ring. Ring.

"Aren't you going to answer that?" the male actor said.

"No," a blonde actress cried. "Everyone who received a call tonight has disappeared or been killed."

Lightning struck in the background, accompanied by the sound of pounding rain. A crack of thunder made her jump.

"Don't be ridiculous," the man smirked.

"Wait!" the actress yelled. The camera fixated on the jiggle of her breasts when she made any movement. "We don't have any reception. I haven't been able to make a call since we arrived here. Why did we come to this place?"

"Relax," the actor answered. "This is a landline. It doesn't need a signal like our cell phones do. See?" he pointed to an antique rotary-style phone sitting alone on a side table. "Answer the call."

The telephone continued to ring.

"Let it ring," she begged, wringing up the bottom of her shirt just enough to reveal the glittering jewelry of her belly-button piercing.

"Answer the call," he yelled. "If you don't answer, I will." He sighed at her lack of movement. His large hand snatched receiver from its base. "Who is this?"

"You should have listened to her, Blake," a maniacal voice scoffed. "Now, you're next!" A dial tone sounded.

One hand covered the actor's mouth - the receiver dropped from the other. His eyes focused on nothing. A dead look covered his face.

"What is it?" the curvy blonde asked. She bent over to pick up the receiver. The picture zoomed in on the bottom of her white underwear peeking out from under the short skirt she was wearing.

"We need to call for help," he answered. He snatched the receiver away from her. His finger clicked on buttons several times. "It's dead," he said. He grabbed the cord and followed it to the wall. The plug end lay on the ground. "How could it have never been plugged in?"

He replaced the receiver. The phone rang.

"Aren't you going to answer the call, Blake?" a gruff voice said. "Answer the call. Answer the call. Answer the call."

A blade slashed at him, cutting his shirt.

He screamed.

His heart pounded and breath laboured. He sat up in his bed, drenched in sweat. "It was just a dream," he said. His fingers ran over his stomach, finding the gash in his shirt. He pulled it off and threw it across the room. The camera made sure to catch every possible angle of his muscles.

*****

"Answer the call," Jessica said, mocking the flick.

"I would never answer." Jade made a hood out of her blanket. "I don't understand why so many people answered it. The only smart one was the dumb blonde."

"You said it, not us," Krissy smirked. "There are some similarities between you and her. You even have almost the exact same phone in your office."

Looking down her shirt, she shook her head. "We don't have them in common."

The girls exploded into another round of laughter.

"Krissy's right," Sarah agreed. "There's the whole dreamwalking thing too."

Willow shot the girl a glare. "That wasn't dreamwalking," she muttered.

"It wasn't," Sarah replied, clueless. "It was in his dreams; the bad guy was real; and the stuff that happened to him was real. Isn't that kinda what dreamwalking is about?"

"Not exactly," Willow answered. "You need a dreamwalker to do things in dreams. A person can't just decide to go prancing about other people's dreams. You either have to call or be called by the dreamwalker. That monster didn't have the restrictions normally imposed by the dream world."

"So it couldn't happen?" Jessica asked.

"Not like that, it couldn't," Willow stated.

"Watch out," Jade whispered, her head nodding towards the figure of a boy hiding behind a tree. "Let's grab him when he comes by."

"Boo!" Nathan yelled, jumping out a moment later. Before he could move he found himself stuck in the middle of a pile of girls - all tickling him. Not being able to hold it in any more, he burst into laughter until his sides hurt and tears streamed down his face. He gasped for air, struggling to find a way out.

"Let the boy go," Zsiga commanded in a booming voice. "You girls have had your fun. We'll clean up. Go on inside."

"Why are you offering to clean up?" Sarah asked, folding her arms over her chest.

"It's a better job than figuring out how to help William change diapers," Zsiga joked. "I'm kidding, Willow. Father and son are doing well."

"Okay," Sarah said. "Make sure you clean up good." She landed a fist in Faramund's shoulder on her way past.

The other girls exchanged glances and giggles. Those two were bound to end up a couple one day - as soon as one of them mustered up the nerve to start the conversation.

Jade wrapped her arm around Willow's for the walk back. "Do you have to go?"

"No," Willow answered. "But I want to. William and I spent a long time discussing our future. We both agreed that we want to rebuild our home world. We want to make it the place it was meant to be. A place where guardians can help teach others how to use their powers for the greater good. A place where we can bring up Lance in peace."

"I'll miss you," Jade sniffled. The moonlight caught a lone tear, drizzling from the corner of her eye, turning it blue.

"We won't be that far away," Willow offered. She wiped the wetness from her friend's face. "It's just a step through the portal to visit."

"You'll be in a different realm," Jade cried, breaking their arm link. "We won't see each other as much. You'll be busy with your family."

"And you'll be busy with your work," Willow said, "and Gavin." Her elbow nudged Jade's side a couple of times.

"Gavin's been on a mission for my dad for a few months now," Jade said, pulling away from her friends jesting. "Somewhere in a jungle checking out some strange energy readings." She sighed. "Dad's busy with the election - re-writing legislation. I just feel like everything is changing."

"Because it is," Willow stated. "I think that's a part of growing up. We all have things that are important to us that we have to do. It doesn't mean we aren't friends anymore. It simply means we have less time to hang out. I'm still there if you need me."

"I wish it wasn't so soon. I already feel alone."

"You'll be fine," Willow said. "You picked this world to make your home in because you love it here. Believe in yourself. Step up and answer the call."

"I can't believe you said that," Jade said, laughing.

"I can't either," Willow spit out in between chuckles. "It was pretty corny. Don't forget Shelby and Lasel are staying with you."

"I'm sure Ashlyn and Clarity will be thrilled to find out," Jade said.

"William had them transferred to a mental hospital designed especially for magical beings. We don't know if either of them will fully recover. I meant to ask you if you could visit once in a while. We'd take them home with us, but Micca made us realise we aren't capable of providing proper care yet. Once we've rebuilt, we'll be back for them."

12

"Ow," Jade said, grabbing her stomach.

"You okay?"

"Yeah," Jade winced. "I think I ate too much popcorn."

Chapter Two

Russ pulled a white cloth from his back pocket. "Who knew vampires could sweat this much," he complained, dabbing the perspiration from his forehead and neck. Hot wasn't nearly a strong enough word for the temperature. "You'd think we were standing at the gates of hell."

Gavin huffed a chuckle without looking up.

"Pretty messed up over that one - aren't you?" Naomi smiled, peeking over his shoulder at the picture her ex-boyfriend couldn't stop staring at. She sighed. "You never looked at me like that."

"And that's just a picture," Russ joked. "Imagine if the mayor's daughter was actually here. I bet he'd be all love-sick and googly-eyed." He laughed.

"Laughing will make you feel the heat more," Gavin warned, the tips of what could be described as fangs visible.

"Really?" Russ' upper lip curved upward, forming an arch.

Naomi laughed. "I have some property I'd like to sell you too," she teased, sidestepping the sweat-covered cloth that hurled at her.

"How long are we going to stay here without finding anything?" Delphine asked.

"As long at the good old mayor keeps paying," Russ stated.

"Watch it," Gavin ordered. "Malarchy is trying to put laws into place to protect our race and give us equal rights. You should be more supportive."

"You sure it's the mayor you are defending?" Naomi asked. "I think that green-eyed monster has you twisted around her finger."

"If anyone is jealous," he scoffed, "it's you." He chuckled at her hissing noises.

An explosion sounded, followed by a noise only falling rocks could make. Workers scattered, running to take any transportation they could.

"Looks like they found something," Russ said.

"Grab someone and find out what the commotion is about," Gavin commanded. "Don't let them steal all the vehicles." He pointed at a mini traffic jam forming. "That's not something you see every day in the jungle." He headed towards the spot the blast came from. "Did we use explosives today?" he yelled back, not slowing his pace.

"Nope," Russ answered. "Too many rocks in those caves. It would have been way too dangerous."

"Well," Gavin said. "Something exploded. If it didn't come from us, where did it come from?" He stopped at the foot of the cave.

"You aren't afraid of a few falling pebbles, are you?" Naomi smirked. "I liked you better when you were the bad boy - tame doesn't suit you." She allowed her shoulder to make contact with his as she pushed past him.

"I thought you were securing our ride," Gavin yelled at her back.

"Delphine has it covered."

"I don't know about you, but I'm not letting her have all the fun," Russ chuckled.

A glow illuminated their eyes. Night vision was one of the more useful perks of being a vampire. Gavin ducked - some dirt and a few pebbles showered down on his head. He was still brushing bits off his shoulders when they caught up to Naomi.

"What do you make of this?" she asked, nodding to a breach in the cave's wall. She ran her fingers across the jagged edges of rock on either side of the fissure. An orange glow radiated from the other side of the gap.

"I can't see anything from this angle," Gavin said, peeking through.

"She can't help you here," Naomi scowled.

He chuckled. Still clenched tight in his hand was Jade's picture. "Thanks," he said, stuffing it into his back pocket. A cracking noise came from his neck as it shifted from side to side. "That's better." One leg slid through the space with ease. The palms of his hands pushed on the rock in front of him as his body wiggled trying to pass through. "No dice." Squirming his way back out proved to be more difficult than he anticipated. He chuckled at the ripping noises, imagining his clothes as cheese being shredded by a grater. A layer of skin became jealous and joined in.

"Ah!" he screamed, prying his body out and falling to the ground. "This outfit has seen better days," he mused, brushing off as much dirt as possible.

"Hate to have to tell you," Naomi chuckled. "But your girlfriend's picture didn't make it. Whatever is on the other side of this wall has it now."

Gavin felt his backside. The whole pocket was gone. "Great," he huffed under his breath. Another rock shower coated him in soot.

18

"Let's get out of here. At the very least, Malarchy will need to send someone who can put a magic seal on the ceiling before we can go any further." A grinding stone-on-stone noise came from above. Gavin glanced up and was rewarded by a layer of dirt on his face. "What is that?" he asked, spitting out a mouth full of small pebbles.

"Looks like a complex dial of some sort," Russ replied, snapping a couple of pictures. "We can let Malarchy help decipher them."

"I was about to come find you," Delphine said. A man's body came to a rolling stop at their feet at the entrance to the cave. "He's the last one. Everyone else is long gone. I managed to save one jeep."

The man took a praying position. "Please," he begged, his hands together in front of his bowed head. "We have unleashed the curse."

"Curse?" Gavin asked, his eyes alternating between Delphine and the worker. "What curse?"

"There is an ancient legend in these parts about the God of Light sealing away the God of Darkness in a mountain," Delphine explained. "They think we somehow caused a breach in that seal."

Seven bat-like creatures swooshed out of the cave in a triangle shaped formation. Naomi ducked as they brushed passed her. In a flash, they disappeared into the cover of the surrounding trees and foliage.

"The seals have escaped." The man's trembling reflected in the sound of his words. "As they are broken, the evil that dwells within the mountain will gain power."

"And ... let me guess - escape," Gavin snickered.

"No," the worker answered. "A choice has been made - a baby will be born. Together, parent and child will have the power to turn the sun dark. Evil will walk freely once more."

"Great," Gavin muttered. "More evil."

"How exactly do we stop the seals for being broken?" Russ asked.

"Seven will become Mornyx's army. Each seal will possess the body and soul of someone who can impact the life of the Chosen One. I know of no way to stop the process."

The sound of rocks crashing down stole the vampires' attention just long enough for the man to scramble to his feet. He bolted to the cave opening and headed into the jungle, his arms failing in front of him.

"Let him go," Gavin said. "I don't think his limited knowledge is going to help us any. We need to check out the local lore on all of this."

"You don't actually buy into all this, do you?" Naomi scoffed.

"After what I have seen in the past year, nothing would surprise me," Gavin answered. "We know there is magic of some sort coming from this cave. This is the closest we have come to even a partial answer since we have been here. I think we need to follow the leads and see where they take us."

"How, exactly, do we do that?" Delphine asked.

"You two girls take the jeep. Check out the local towns for any information you can find about the God of Darkness and the God of Light. Maybe we'll get lucky and find something."

"What about you two?" Delphine asked.

"We'll stay here and watch the site." Gavin answered. "No sense leaving it unattended. I don't want a bunch of terunji thrill seekers showing up and getting themselves trapped in a rock slide. We don't need that sort of attention."

Chapter Three

Ring. Ring. Ring.

"Answer the call."

Ring. Ring. Ring.

"Step up and answer the call!"

Jade bolted upright. Sweat trickled from her neck down her back, adding more moisture to her already soaked nightgown. The pounding of her heart throbbed in her head. She rubbed her temples, hoping to relieve the pressure before the beating returned to normal. After a few minutes of deep breathing, she calmed down.

It was just a dream, she thought. That movie had hit a nerve and stuck with her. Ever since seeing it, the same dream plagued her sleep. The phone rang over and over. In the background, a muffled voice yelled, *answer the call.* Of course, she ignored the words, choosing to try to cover her ears to stop the ringing. It was silly when all the actors answered the phone and ended up victims. There was no way she would ever make the same mistake they did.

Her feet crept out from under the covers, not anxious to touch the cold floor. It was almost morning. There was little point heading back to bed. If she fell asleep now, she never would have been awake on time for work - even with her alarm set on the highest volume. She yawned.

I could use a few hours' sleep without any dreams, she thought.

Are they that troublesome? Shelby asked. *We are here, if you want to talk.*

Maybe later, she replied. The truth was, she did want to talk. She wanted to pull Willow back from her new life and make her stay. She wanted Gavin to return from his expedition and be there for her. She wanted her father to finish his election work and spend time with her. She wanted a friend; a confident; and most importantly, she didn't want to be alone. None of that was going to happen anytime soon. As for the two guardians, perhaps, one day she would be able to share all her fears with them, but she wasn't ready yet.

Becoming a keeper had been so natural for the others. William; Clarity; Ashlyn; and even Nick had all effortlessly transitioned. Somehow, it seemed unnatural for her. That feeling created a world of problems for the three in attempting to coexist. There wasn't a steady telepathic link or a bond strong enough to form an unbreakable trust. Those were things they needed to work on. Those were things she told herself would come in time.

For now, burying herself in work was the best plan she had. At least if she was busy, there was little chance of falling asleep again.

She examined herself in a full-length mirror as she dressed. Pictures of the two black birds were prominently displayed on her shoulder blades. She chose a blouse that covered their view completely.

Was that necessary? Shelby asked.

It would be hard to explain to my co-workers why I have pictures of birds that move around daily. The war with Cornelius may be over, but Kasper Deogole still hasn't forgotten the grudge he has against Willow. Now that she is gone, I would be a prime target for his frustration if someone was to suggest I was carrying guardians.

I suppose you have a point, Shelby conceded.

A knock at the door could only mean one thing; Constable Safron Black was there to escort her to work. She swung a jacket over her shoulder and grabbed her briefcase on the way out.

"Good Morning, Jade," Safron said, twirling the end of one half of his moustache upwards. "I trust you slept well."

"Good morning," she muttered back, ignoring the last part of the man's greetings. She put on a pair of sunglasses; partly to cover the bags under her eyes and partly to block out the bright orange and yellow of the constable's suit. "If you don't mind, I'd like to go straight to the office today."

"Of course," Safron replied. "I have a feeling it's going to be an extraordinary day."

She didn't share in his sentiments.

Chapter Four

"I thought you might want this," Esmerelda said, "what with your father having his big speech today and all." A portable television set plopped on her desk with a thud. Reaching into her blue beehive coiffure, she pulled out a remote.

"Esmeralda," Jade said. "Why is there a rabbit on top of it?"

"Rabbit's ears, of course," she answered. "They get the best reception. The signal is coming from the other side of the world."

Jade nodded. "Thank you," she said. "How long do I have before it starts?"

"Don't worry about that," Esmerelda insisted. "I'll come back and make sure it's on so you don't miss a thing." A pink bubble protruded from between her lips before popping back to join the rest of the wad of gum perpetually churning in her mouth. "If you don't mind, I'll watch a bit with you. The main office is closing up to cheer on the mayor."

"Of course," Jade replied. "I'd actually love the company."

"Perfect," Esmerelda squealed in her usual nasal sound. "I'll be back." The door shut behind her.

Jade turned her attention back to the papers on her desk. The words faded into each other - her vision blurring.

Ring. Ring. Ring.

"Answer the call! Jade, answer the call!"

Jade's head lifted off her desk. She ran her hand across her mouth, wiping away the residue of drool. *Sleep*, she thought, *I must have fallen asleep again.*

Ring. Ring. Ring.

"Answer the call!" Esmerelda yelled. "Honestly, Jade, with your father gone, you need to step up and answer the calls that come in."

Jade shook her head. This wasn't a dream. The receiver was already hovering by her ear. "Hello," she said.

"Oh, Jade, darling," Delilah said. "How are you? We haven't spoken in some time. I thought I'd drop you a line and let you know we'll all be watching. Even my daughter, Prudance, is coming here tonight. I know your father will do great things."

"Thank you," Jade muttered, still shaking off sleepiness.

"You wouldn't happen to know his position on the elite status of multi-generation families, would you?" the woman asked, her voice raising a few octaves at the end of her question.

"I'm sorry, Delilah," Jade answered. "You will have to watch his speech with everyone else. I wish I could tell you, but not even I have heard it yet."

"I see," Delilah snarled. "You can understand our concern, with all the rumours about you and a vampire being a couple. Of course, that simply isn't true."

Jade held the receiver away from her ear for a moment and sucked in a large breath of air. After her lungs were saturated to capacity she released it again and returned to the on-going conversation.

"Imagine the horror the upscale community had when we heard all this," Delilah shrieked.

"I don't believe my personal life is anyone's business."

"Of course it is," Delilah disagreed. "Especially if it makes your father more lenient towards those sort that don't have a place in our community."

"By those sort, you mean the vamprite?" Jade asked.

"For starters, yes."

"I see," Jade said. "I assure you I have no control over my father's policies. They are decided on his own. Thank you for calling, Delilah, and have a good day."

"Well, I've never..."

The phone went dead, just like in the movie. Jade grasped her sides and keeled over in her chair. She winced. Pain - the same pain she had felt when she last saw Willow, but stronger. Something was wrong.

*****

"I brought some popcorn and chocolate," Esmerelda said, walking in. "Jade, are you alright?"

Jade's head lifted. The pain was finally subsiding. How long had she been huddled over? Had it been hours?

"I'll be okay," Jade lied. "I'm a bit tired. I haven't been sleeping well."

"It's no wonder with all that is going on," Esmerelda replied, setting the food down on the desk. "You must be stressed. I know I would be if my father was about to make waves in the magic community."

"Thanks for that," Jade said, forcing a smile. She hadn't actually thought about the fallout that would happen after today's speech aired. Truth was, no one actually new what would happen after he lobbied for equal rights.

"It's about to start," Esmerelda pointed out. She turned up the volume on the small screen and adjusted the rabbit's ears. "Look, there he is. My, the Mayor does look handsome."

Jade side-eyed the woman. In her mind, no one had the right to think of her father in that way. She sighed as she watched him take his place on the stage. Esmerelda was right. He did look handsome. Everything in her life was changing; maybe it wasn't just in her life.

"Good evening," Malarchy said.

His speech began with a few well-received jokes before turning to serious issues. All the usual topics one might expect from a politician were covered: safety; jobs; unity; communication; and education. Then everything went quiet - not just on the screen, but in the office as well. This was the part everyone was waiting for. This was what was going to change the future.

A glass of ice water lifted to the mayor's lips. The only thing sweating was the glass. If he was nervous, it wasn't showing. He paused for a moment, allowing his gaze to glance back at his new personal assistant Aurora.

A smile crossed Jade's lips. She knew exactly what her father was doing. As talented at illusion as Malarchy was, his true gift, the one only a few people knew about, was persuasion. With Aurora feeding him her energy, he was a force to be reckoned with. Maybe it would be enough to win him this election.

"Equality," Malarchy started, "is not a privilege afforded to the elite. It's a fundamental right we are all born with. It doesn't matter where we were born, what we look like, or what we believe in. We are all individuals. If we are to coexist in this realm as one, there needs to be a policy in effect to protect the rights of each and every citizen residing in any of our beautiful cities. I intend to make this a priority if I am elected to office. You can expect to see immediate changes, including: fair pay; equal access to government programs; more minorities in government positions; and standardized laws and rules for everyone. Special rights based on heritage or birthright will become a thing of the past."

A grumble exploded - a mixture of cheers and boos, so evenly matched, it was impossible to tell which was louder. The phones rang and didn't stop for the rest of the day. Malarchy was being hailed both a hero and a traitor.

"I think it would be best if Safron escorted you home early," Esmerelda suggested. "Pewterclaw is home to many of those your father alienated with that speech."

"He hasn't actually been elected yet," Jade pointed out.

"It doesn't matter, dear," Esmerelda replied. "He has made some powerful enemies." She lowered her voice to a whisper. "Some of them are right here, in this building. Tempers are running high right now. Take the rest of the day off and stay at home."

That advice was sound. How could she refuse?

Chapter Five

Jade rushed to the door. "Thanks for coming over," she said, hugging the two girls. "I haven't been able to sleep since we watched that movie." She froze on the spot. The colour drained from her face. "What is he doing here?" she demanded.

"This isn't exactly where I want to spend my night either," Simon said, pushing passed her. He plopped down on the couch, stretching his legs out, eliminating the chance anyone could sit beside him. It was impossible to tell he had never stepped foot in that apartment before. His perfectly chiselled body looked completely at home.

If Jade hadn't met his two older brothers, she wasn't sure if she would have been surprised to hear he was considered the runt of the princes. Not only his devilishly good-looking appearance, but also an undeniable charisma created an unmistakable allure. She wanted to like him and, under different circumstances, she might have.

Krissy linked arms with Jade. "You said you were having nightmares. Who better to help than a dreamwalker?"

"Can we trust him?" Jade whispered. Thinking back, she wasn't sure things had ever been resolved with the survivors of Conelius' offspring.

"A dreamwalker with good hearing," Simon blurted out. "I didn't have to come."

"He's changed," Krissy explained. "Lance's death really affected him. Things are different. It's up to all of us to ... answer the call." She giggled. "Ow," she cried. A punch in the arm was probably deserved, but Jade could have used a little less force.

"Not funny," Jade pouted. "These dreams are bad. They are driving me crazy."

"So," Simon said. "Let me try to help you. If they are caused by another dreamwalker, we can put an end to it."

"I don't know," Jade answered. She gripped her sides, the pain she felt before returning. This was becoming too regular a feeling for her to be coincidence.

"Are you okay?" Jessica asked.

"I'm fine," Jade replied. "I think the popcorn and sweets are getting to me." She turned away, hoping to conceal any information that might be given away by the expression on her face about the lie she had just told.

"Look," Simon pleaded. "If there is some plot twisting to take over the world, I want to stop it. I'm a part of this realm now too."

"Who said anything about taking over the world?" Jade asked.

Jessica sighed. "When something weird happens to one of you, there is usually a connection to some sinister plot."

That was hard to argue with, but also something Jade hadn't considered. "Sometimes a dream is just a dream," she explained, not entirely sure who she was trying to convince - her guests, or herself.

"No," Simon replied. "Dreams are always something more than we care to admit. Whether you are meant to heed their warnings or someone is invading them, they all have purpose. That is why we don't dream every night. If your dreams are as bad as you say, you need help."

"We'll be going too," Krissy exclaimed with her usual zeal. She dripped with enthusiasm, accentuated even further by laughing monkeys printed all over her pink pyjamas. "The four of us can figure this out."

"Look at you," Jessica added. She was as polar opposite to Krissy as could be possible. Her blue, pin-striped suit screamed anything but sleepover. "You're a wreck. You can't go on like this much longer. Trust us. We'll go in figure out what's going on and get out fast."

"Alright," Jade said. "I'll grab some pillows and blankets. I have to warn you though, some of the images you will see are disturbing."

"I doubt anything could be more disturbing than the horrors I have seen while awake. I think you forget the brutality my father was capable of."

"I believe you forget that you were once a party to that brutality as well," Jade answered.

"Touché." Simon responded, making a circular motion with his hand in front of his slightly bowed head.

Chapter Six

Ring. Ring. Ring. Ring.

"Answer the call," Simon demanded.

"I," Jade stuttered, "I don't want to."

"Answer the call," Simon repeated.

Jade didn't move.

"Answer the call," Krissy said.

"Answer the call," Jessica echoed.

"I don't want to!" Jade yelled. Her body cowered into a squatting position, her arms covering her face and head. She felt a hand on her shoulder and peeked up.

"If we are going to move forward in this dream and find out who or what is behind it, we need you to answer the call," Simon explained. He extended a hand to help her up.

Jade nodded. Her lungs filled with air. She clenched her eyes closed. Somehow the receiver found its way to her ear. "Hello," she said.

"Have you finally found the nerve to do what you have to do?" an eerie voice on the other end asked. It wasn't a voice she had heard before and yet it had a distinct familiarity to it that couldn't be pinpointed.

"What is it I have to do?" Jade questioned after a few moments.

"Save the world, of course," the voice cackled. "But I'm not sure you are even capable of saving yourself and your friends." More laughter followed. Not a regular laugh, but rather a generic sinister laugh one might expect to hear in a poorly made movie.

"I don't know what to do!" Jade cried.

"Look around you, girl," the voice demanded, now deeper and with force. "The clues are written. Follow your destiny. Save the ones you love and you will save the world. There is no room for failure." The phone went dead.

"Over there," Simon said, pointing.

"Are those," Jessica queried, "puppets?"

The group inched closer to a gathering of wooden dolls supported by strings. Simon reached out to touch the first one. He jumped backwards when it began to move.

"I thought you were the master of dreams," Jessica snarled.

Simon side-glanced his disapproval at her. "Shock value. I didn't expect it to move."

"Where is it going?" Jade asked.

"To answer that question," Simon said, pushing passed the others to take the lead, "we follow."

"What's it doing?" Krissy asked, peering out from behind Simon's tall frame.

"It seems to be carving something in stone."

The three girls popped their heads from behind Simon, just enough to see the puppet work. All three let out a scream as a second wooden figure passed by to join the other.

"There are seven circular slabs on the wall. That's one for each puppet," Simon said. "Maybe they are carving a message of some sort? We need to get closer."

"Are you sure that's a good idea?" Jade asked. She had been frightened when they stood in a plain dark room with a telephone, but now their surroundings had morphed into something even more disturbing. The very air they breathed was filled with the fright of a horror movie, accentuated by dark grey walls, a low lying mist and a general sense of foreboding evil.

"Don't let it get to you," Simon said. "None of this is real. I can change the scenery in a flash if I need to."

The group inched closer. Puppets three and four were now working beside their predecessors. Jade and her three companions stood motionless, watching over the shoulder of one of the life-sized mannequin etching stone with precision.

"Is that a picture of a dog?" Krissy asked, her nose scrunching up. "Not much of an artist, is he?"

Simon glanced sideways at her before shaking his head. "He is a doll. What did you expect? I think we should concentrate on what the word is he seems to be writing."

The etchings began to glow - a soft white light at first - then it began to darken, taking on a green shade – a jade green.

"Envy?" Jade asked.

Her words were followed by the sound of grinding stone. Above them, lodged in the ceiling was a stone dial, similar to a watch, except with only eight places instead of twelve on the outer ring. Each one imprinted with a symbol of an animal. An arrow hand moved from the starting point to rest upon one symbol. The inner ring spun at a rate too fast to see if there were any markings on it. Another stone crushing noise and a crack in the ceiling formed around the dial.

"It looks like a doorway of some sort is opening," Simon said, brushing off some dust that had landed on his black suit.

"But to where?" Jessica asked. "Do you think we are supposed to go through?"

"No," Simon answered. "I think something is trying to get out. The puppets appear to be keys to opening the larger dial. Once all seven have completed, whatever is locked up will be free."

"Why are only four working?" Jade asked.

"No clue," Simon replied.

"Have we seen enough?" Krissy asked, rubbing her shoulders. "I have a bad feeling about being here when they finish."

"I'll agree with that," Jessica said.

Jade darted a glance at the two girls. "You two are the ones who wanted to see my dream in the first place."

"And we've seen it," Krissy said. "Simon..."

Simon pressed his lips together, remaining silent.

"Simon!" Jessica exclaimed.

"Whoever is controlling this dream isn't a dreamwalker," he answered.

"What exactly does that mean?" Jade asked.

"This isn't a dream realm. As far as I can tell, it is another dimension. I have no power here." Simon replied.

"How long have you known?!" Jessica demanded.

"Since the puppet caught me off-guard," he admitted. "That isn't something that could have happened in an actual dream."

"And when were you going to let us in on that tidbit of information?" Jessica asked, one foot tapping.

"I didn't see any reason to alarm you any more than necessary," Simon explained. "I had a theory that when the message was finished we would automatically be transported back to the apartment."

"So we are stuck here?!" Krissy squealed.

"I think Jade is able to take us back out," Simon said.

Jade shook her head. She had no idea what to do. Rescuing them was supposed to be Simon's job - that's why he was there in the first place. She inhaled deeply. There was no choice but to try. She closed her eyes tight. When she opened them again, they were back in her apartment, safe - for the moment.

Chapter Seven

"Why didn't you contact me sooner?!" Malarchy yelled, a red flush creeping over his face like a shadow.

"You have the election and the new legislation to worry about," Jade answered. "I didn't want to add any more on top." She paused for a moment. "I wanted to believe it all stemmed from that movie I watched. Until tonight, I didn't believe it was real." She chomped down on her thumbnail that had found its way between her lips.

"This is serious!" Malarchy exclaimed. "We have seen countless times how dangerous the dream world can be."

"Not exactly the dream world," Simon interrupted.

"Why is he here?" Malarchy asked, raising an eyebrow. "Last I heard, we were on opposite sides."

"Now, that isn't fair," Simon said. "I thought you were all for equality for everyone. I am a part of this world too, after all. Besides, it isn't possible for me to go back to the life I once had, so I figure I might as well start a new one - if you can't beat them, join them. I believe that's the correct saying. You could at least give me credit for trying to help your daughter. That should count for something."

"Wonderful," Malarchy replied. "Seems we have a new brother to contend with."

"That's low," Simon scowled. "Regardless of what you think of my brothers, they are still family. Lance will be missed."

"He might be closer than you think," Krissy mumbled followed by a snort.

Sarah coughed and shook her head. This wasn't the time or the place to try to explain to the prince that his brother had been reincarnated.

"Very discreet," Simon spit out. His feet landed with a thud on Gavin's desk. The chair suited him, or perhaps it was the office in general. "I'm not sure what you think you know about my brother's demise, but I assure you he is very much dead."

"What we know is that apparently we are stuck with you." Malarchy pushed Simon's feet to the ground. "This desk, however, isn't yours."

Simon laughed. "You are indeed stuck with me," he jested, brushing his dark hair off of his face in an eerily natural motion. For a moment Jade wondered if he had considered doing shampoo commercials. One simple motion of his hand had layered red highlights perfectly for optimal exposure amongst the natural black base of his hair.

"So why don't you make yourself useful?" Malarchy asked. "Tell us what you know."

The chair wheeled closer to the desk. Simon leaned forward, clasping his hands together in front of him. "The dream world is a place that is but isn't at the same time. Unlike worlds divided by portals that exist on one plain, dreams exist in another place. What happens there is real and yet not real. When someone enters a dream, they are there and yet their physical body remains anchored in the here and now."

Malarchy huffed. "Your brother fully explained this to us already."

"Did you want my help?" Simon asked. "I can stop anytime."

"My apologies," Malarchy said, his words dripping with sarcasm, "please continue."

Simon smiled, exposing perfect white teeth. Moving his hands behind his head, he leaned back in the chair and placed his feet back on the desk - issuing a personal challenge to knock them off again. "Call off your muscle," he snarled as he side-eyed Faramund inching closer.

Malarchy nodded at the guard.

"Although the dream world is another place, it is on a mental plane. The place we were in was somewhere between the mental and physical worlds." Simon's feet fell to the ground. The chair scooted forward. "I know you understand that there is a way for spirits to contact the living through dreams. You have experienced it. Some of your people have experienced it. I know, I was there. In an actual dream spirit communication is limited: symbols; smells; and simple phrases. It's actually quite pathetic. This isn't that either."

Malarchy threw his hands in the air. "Brilliant," he said. "Any chance you could tell us what it is?"

"The place Jade goes is a combination of all three: the physical realm; the mental realm; and the spirit realm. In essence, it is a new dimension." Simon clapped his hands together. "It's truly amazing - revolutionary stuff - very cutting edge."

"But where did it come from?" Jade asked.

"Something very powerful created it," Simon answered. "I don't know if it is whatever is behind that lock or something else.

Whoever or whatever created it has a message for Jade. I don't think it will stop until everything it has to say has been not only heard, but also understood."

"So," Krissy said, "what do we do?"

"Obviously we aren't doing well with interpreting the message," Sarah said, pushing the glasses up the bridge of her nose. "If this entity is powerful enough to create a new dimension to try to communicate through, I think it is safe to say it is intelligent. Whoever it is must realize Jade is coming up blank in the interpretation department. Most likely there will be an alternate attempt to communicate."

"You are suggesting we simply wait?" Krissy asked. "That would be like offering Jade up as bait."

"Great," Jade moaned. "I was already scared to fall asleep. Now I have something else to worry about."

"Don't forget," Simon added, "you were chosen for this message. That suggests whatever is going on has a connection to you."

"Basically what you are saying is we know that something is going to happen and Jade is involved," Jessica said.

"What we don't know," Simon offered, "is if the entity is sending a warning to help or ..."

"Or," Jade interrupted, "a prediction of what's to come."

Chapter Eight

It wasn't the dream that woke Jade that evening. The room itself shook her back to reality. She surveyed the damage from where she sat. When she sat down behind Gavin's desk, she had been looking for comfort - to find a feeling of the man she missed more and more with passing day. She hadn't expected to fall asleep, albeit she was exhausted.

Jade blinked twice, trying to adjust her eyes to the darkness. Her hand reached for the remote control she had programmed herself especially for Gavin. One of the little things she did to try to make him more comfortable - one of the things he hadn't noticed. She pressed the button for the lights. One of the bulbs from the light fixture attached to the ceiling began to hum - it flashed on and off a few times before remaining lit.

"Are you alright?!" Krissy yelled from the doorway. "The whole place shook."

"I think," Jessica said, "that was an earthquake." She pushed passed the others and took a seat on the couch.

"I didn't know earthquakes could happen in Pewterclaw," Krissy muttered while scribbling notes on a small pad of paper.

"They can't," Simon replied. "That, whatever it was, wasn't an earthquake."

Jade paid little attention to the conversation going on, her vision fixated on an arch of pretty colours that had formed as a result of the light shining through the broken light fixture. Simon was quick to pick up on what caused her distraction.

"How interesting," he said, "a rainbow. You know, it's said there is a treasure hidden at the end - if you can find it."

"Really!" Jade exclaimed. A twinkle that had been absent from her eyes for some time returned, accompanied by a smile. She stood and followed the band of colours to where it disappeared on a shelf behind a familiar book. Her fingers shook as they traced the spine of the book that used to be *The Portal Prophecies*. She gulped back the saliva pooling in her mouth and pulled it out. A layer of dust floated up in the air accentuated by the lighting. The rainbow disappeared.

"I thought all the words were erased from that book," Krissy said, tiptoeing and stretching her neck. "Seems like a terrible treasure."

"You do know you look ridiculous, right?" Simon asked. "You can't actually see inside by changing your position."

The young reporter's eyebrows pushed together, forming frown lines to match the pout that had already graced her lips. "I know that," she snapped. "I can't help it. Reporters are curious creatures. It's a natural instinct."

"To be fair," Jessica offered, "the treasure at the end of a rainbow is thought to belong to leprechauns and be a pot of gold."

"Leprechauns!" Sarah exclaimed.

"Have you been standing there this whole time?" Jessica asked.

"Never mind that," Sarah answered. "Are leprechauns real?"

"Maybe," Simon replied. "I've never actually met one, but from what I have heard many of the stories of this world are backed by some form of reality." A toothy smile accentuated his already handsome appearance. There was something unnatural about being that good looking after being shaken out of bed. He fired off a quick wink.

Red crept up into Jessica's face. She cleared her throat. "We have been discussing some unusual findings from this world - for speculation as to the current events."

"Uh-huh," Krissy said, side-eyeing the two.

"So, am I to understand that another of Cornelius' sons has captured the trust of a member of my team with his charm?" Malarchy said, pushing into the room. "I was here to see if everyone was alright after the unusual tremor, but this is much more fascinating." He chuckled without cracking even a hint of a grin. If anyone hadn't known he was being sarcastic when he spoke, they definitely did after that. "Does Kasper know?"

"There is nothing to know!" Jessica yelled. She shrugged her shoulders and bit her bottom lip. "Sorry. I didn't mean to be so loud."

"Indeed," Malarchy said, arching an eyebrow.

Jade never heard a word of the squabbling going on around her. The book was all that mattered. Her fingers traced the cover where words used to be and new ones appeared. "Jade's Gurney." Her rose crinkled up. "What does that mean?"

The book slid around to face Simon. "That's what it says - Jade's Gurney. Maybe it's a new hospital romance?" he mused.

"You don't think it's a prediction you'll need a gurney, do you?" Krissy asked.

"We could open it and find out," Malarchy said, grabbing the book. His thumb flipped through the pages. *Beware! The want; the craving; the addiction; the apathy; the rage; the jealousy; and the vein.* "Apparently, we've been graced with a prophet who can't spell. What luck."

"No! No! No!" a voice bellowed. A puff of smoke and a tiny man, no bigger than six inches tall, appeared on the desk. He paced back and forth holding one finger in the air. "I have to be the one who is stuck with an age-old request. It could have been any leprechaun, but no."

"Excuse me," Jade said. "Who are you?"

"Who am I? Who am I?" The man echoed, moving closer to the edge of the desk. "You don't know?" He bent forward from the waist and stared at Jade. His head tilted to one side as he straightened up again. "Well, of course you don't know. We haven't met yet – officially, that is. Allow me to introduce myself. I am Tobias Shemus William Murtogh O'Sullivan the 93rd, at your service." He bowed. "But me friends call me Toby."

"Well, Toby," Simon started.

"I said me friends call my Toby. You sir, are not me friend and may call me Tobias Shemus William Murtogh O'Sullivan."

"You expect me to use your whole name?"

"I left out the 93rd," Toby replied.

Simon rolled his eyes. "Wonderful."

"Tobias Shemus ..."

"My lovely," Toby interrupted, "you may call me Toby. A delicate flower as perfect as you should be cared for and watered daily."

"There will be no watering of my daughter!" Malarchy bellowed.

"I meant no disrespect," Tobias said, removing his hat to address Jade's father. Curly red hair fell down around his face, matching his long bushy beard.

"Perhaps we could get back to the issue at hand?" Malarchy asked.

"Perhaps someone should grab the little critter before he gets away," Simon sneered. "Isn't there a prize for catching one?"

Toby jumped backwards, his arms flailed around as he teetered on the edge of the desk, before falling into Jade's hand.

"Careful!" she cried. "We almost needed a gurney for you."

"It's journey, not gurney," Toby said. He sat down on a pile of papers. His hat turned in circles between his fingers. "I've gone and done it now. I'm indebted to you. If I weren't so much of a klutz, I wouldn't be here in the first place. I haven't fulfilled my last master's wish and her I am owing more."

"Wish?" Jessica asked. "I thought it was gold at the end of the rainbow."

"You leave me gold out of it. It belongs to me. I worked hard for every piece. I only have to give up my treasure if I fail to perform a task for a master - them's the rules."

"So I get a wish?" Jade asked.

"Three of 'em."

"They can be anything?"

"I did mention there are some rules," Toby answered. "You can't wish for more wishes; you can't override a previous wish by someone else; it must relate to you in some way, so no world peace; I cannot reverse time, ageing or death; and I must warn you everything comes with a price. That's important. I cannot undo a deed once it is done. Any consequences that attach itself to fulfilling your wishes are permanent."

"So she could ask you what in the realms is going on?" Malarchy barked.

"No," Toby answered, "afraid not. That would be breaking a previous task."

"Can you tell us who gave you that task?" Simon pried.

"Um. No."

"So, there is some sort of leprechaun-master privileged information code?" Krissy asked.

Tobias stared at her for a moment before answering. "No. I simply don't know. It was a long time ago and he only wanted one task done. He wished the same wish three times and threw in some gold. I am bound to finishing his request as he set it out."

"You can't tell us," Sarah interrupted, "but if we guessed, you wouldn't be doing anything wrong. Couldn't you disagree if we were wrong and say nothing if we guess correctly?"

"I suppose," Tobias started, "that wouldn't be breaking any rules. Yes, I think I could handle that. Ye wouldn't happen to have a spot of whisky for an ole man to sip on while we play this game, would ye? I'm a bit parched."

The wall creaked. Malarchy looked at the remote in his hand and pressed another button - a bar appeared. "I'm not sure what to do for a cup," he said.

"The cap'll do," Toby answered. "You might not be as bad as I thought." He accepted the cap full of liquor from the mayor. "Ah! You go ahead and call me Toby."

"I'm truly honoured," Malarchy replied, rolling his eyes.

"Best leave the bottle," Tobias requested. "If you are planning on trying to guess the past, we are going to be here a very long time."

"You assume," Krissy said, "we aren't smart enough to figure this out. I think we can make a strong case against that."

"Right," Toby said, gulping down the rest of the cap full. "Shall someone else start then?"

"This man must have known Jade was going to be involved," Simon said, filling the cap to the brim with another round of whisky.

"Don't think I don't know what you are doing, laddie," Tobias said, eyeing the former prince. "I wasn't born yesterday and I am not gullible enough to be bought by one drink."

"Indeed," Malarchy muttered.

"But you didn't disagree with my statement," Simon said.

Tobias looked away and took another sip.

"Your job was to find her and give her messages periodically." Simon stated with confidence.

"How did you know that?" Tobias questioned.

"That part really isn't scientific," Simon explained. "You were writing in a book for Jade to read. You chose a book rather than a single piece of paper because there was bound to be multiple messages. It also supports some theories I have about Jade's dreams. I believe whoever is behind the new dimension is also the one who tasked our new little friend with contacting Jade."

Tobias gasped.

"If I am correct, there is meant to be one initial message and then an additional, for lack of a better word, prediction for each of the seven wooden puppets we saw. The mystery man is probably not with us anymore, perhaps even the one behind the lock." Simon rubbed his chin. "He probably had to write the messages as vague as possible because he didn't have all the facts of this time.

Something wasn't fixated as destiny amongst the slew of things he knew would be."

"If you know all the answers, what do you need me for?" Tobias asked, crossing his arms.

"We don't know everything," Simon said. "We don't know what the messages are; we don't know who is behind the locks; we don't know if this is a cry for help, or an invitation to disaster; we don't know where all this is going to take place..."

"Actually," Malarchy interrupted, "we do." A handful of pictures floated down, landing on the desk like misaligned pieces to a puzzle. "I received these right before I came here."

"That looks like the dial in my dream!" Jade squealed. "Where did you get them?"

"Gavin sent them," Malarchy answered. "The pictures are too small to see the exact markings."

"Did you try contacting him for better shots?" Simon asked.

Malarchy arched an eyebrow. He snatched the picture from Simon's hand. "Of course I did. I've been playing this game much longer than you have."

Simon rolled his eyes. "So when can we expect to see them?"

"We can't," Malarchy admitted. "I seem to have lost contact with Gavin and his crew. It probably has something to do with the tremor."

"Now you've made the pretty lady sad." Tobias pointed to Jade, her eyes glossed over. "You could go there and check things out yourselves."

Malarchy sighed. "That is the plan. I have sent for Faramund to transport a group of us."

"I'm going!" Jade demanded.

"No, you aren't," Malarchy answered.

"This is about me," Jade argued. "I need to be there."

"And I'll be right with you," Toby interrupted. "In case you want to use on of yer wishes."

"And in case your other master wants to relay a message," Simon added. "I don't trust you, little man, and it isn't because of your green suit or red hair. You work in half-truths. Did you think we'd believe you fell into Jade's hands by accident? Let's cut the act. You needed to stay close to her to fulfil your other obligations and that was the easiest way."

"You're a sly one indeed," Tobias replied. "Regardless of how it happened, I owe the lady three wishes if she chooses to use em. I have no choice but to tag along. I can do it in the shadows or right here where you can see me."

"I'd like to be able to see you," Jade said. "I have a feeling I need all the help I can get."

Chapter Nine

"How far do we have to walk?" Krissy asked, swatting a large, rubbery leaf from her face. "Couldn't Faramund get us closer?" She let out a shriek that caught everyone's attention. "Sorry. I still visualize Hilary's face on every spider I see and that one is rather large and hairy." She pointed to a web that had been hidden behind the foliage.

"And poisonous too," Sarah said. "That's a rare species. If I had more time, I'd take a sample of its venom. I think there might be some similarities between the cross-breeds like Hilary and a handful of spiders natural to this world. That brings us to question if there is a possibility of natural evaluation into guardian forms..." The stares were enough motivation to set aside her lesson for another time - one when they weren't running low on what little daylight was available. Of course, she knew at least one member of her party would have something to say regardless of her actions.

"Fascinating," Malarchy said. "Perhaps you could type that up for some light reading when we aren't in the middle of a jungle?"

"I should do that," Sarah said, placing her hands on her hips. "Sorry. I get carried away sometimes." A branch swung back at her. She ducked, barely missing being hit.

"Why is it so hot?" Krissy whined, wiping the sweat trickling down her face.

Simon shook his head. "Because it's a jungle," he answered. "I suggest we start moving again. We need to reach the campsite before the sun goes down."

"Indeed," Malarchy agreed.

"What happens at night?" Krissy asked.

"There are things more dangerous than spiders at night," Simon answered. "You sure you don't want to let you brother do that leg work on this one?"

"I reserve the right to re-visit that option," Krissy answered. That would be the easy option, to let her brother's persona take over. Of course, that would mean giving up a possible story. She wasn't ready to do that just yet.

"It's not much further," Shelby cawed without landing. "Keep moving and you should be there in the blink of an eye."

Krissy blinked twice. "I'm not there yet," she said, giggling - the only one amused by the joke. "Hey, wait up."

"No waiting," Malarchy said. "And I suggest we stop the chatter. Creatures of the night will be beginning their hunt soon. Unnecessary noise will attract them to us. I'd prefer not to be a nightcrawler's dinner menu."

"No worries," Simon said, squatting down to examine deep tire tracks. "I think we found them - at least whoever is left. Whatever vehicle made these tracks was leaving in a hurry." He removed a crooked black wand from his pocket. "Be on guard."

Jade followed suite. The tiny blonde-wood wand with a green gem tip looked perfectly natural locked in her grasp. She remained silent.

"Say the word if you need a wish," Tobias whispered in her ear. From his seat on her shoulder he had the perfect view of their surroundings.

Shelby landed beside the leprechaun. "I suggest," the bird said, "you don't pressure her into making any hasty choices. I can see every move you make. A bird could easily mistake you for a tasty morsel." She took flight again.

Following the tire tracks made things a bit easier for the group - the foliage was already cleared and a path led directly to the rocky hillside and the makeshift camp.

"Cozy," Krissy said, crinkling up her nose at the semi-circle of tents surrounding a fire pit. "Is anyone even left here?"

"Indeed," Gavin answered. "At least two of us are still here. What brings the troops out from the city?" His lips puckered, preparing to meet Jade's cheek, but were rewarded with a slap.

"Watch where ye be putting them things, laddie. I have no intention of being part of yer undead army," Tobias said.

"Who, or what, is that?" Gavin asked, moving to shake Malarchy's hand.

"A leprechaun," Simon answered.

Gavin spun around and pointed a finger at the prince. "This is an unusual group you are travelling with, Malarchy. Anything you'd like to share?"

"A leprechaun who doesn't know anything about our race," Russ said, "wasn't a part of the deal. Everyone has heard about their kind - the greediest creatures in existence."

"Said the blood-sucking beast," Tobias hissed.

Gavin howled a laugh. "I think you have heard a few too many folk tales. I assure you, we do not suck blood from the necks of unsuspecting maidens, stealing their souls and turning them into the undead." He wiggled his fingers at the small man.

"Perhaps you don't, but that doesn't mean there aren't those who do," Tobias replied, the sides of his lips curled in such a way it was impossible to tell is he was smiling or frowning.

"Are you implying there are other races of vampires we may not be aware of?" Malarchy asked, arching an eyebrow.

"I am indeed," A puff of smoke escaped a tiny pipe that had appeared in his mouth. "Surely a fine group like you can't believe that you know everything. No matter how hard we try, no one will ever be able to solve every mystery. There is always an unknown factor. Take, for instance, these vampires. They both believe they are the only of their type to exist - assuming their kind simply was. But where did they come from? That's the question."

"Are you suggesting the vamprite are a by-product of another species?" Malarchy asked. "One, that was perhaps more similar to the terunji tales?"

"I knew you were a smart one. That is exactly what I am saying."

"An interesting theory," Gavin commented. "But, wouldn't we know if there was an all-powerful being that we were molded after?"

"Perhaps you would," Toby smirked, "but then again, perhaps you wouldn't. How far back does your history go? The official leprechaun records date back before ... er, um ...well, dates."

"I don't suppose we could see those records, could we?" Gavin asked.

"Not physically," Toby answered. "Only leprechauns can actually see the journals, but I could re-read them and report back to you. Of course, M'Lady would need to use one of her wishes."

"How kind of you," Simon retorted.

"It's me job. Don't shame me for that," Toby barked back.

"Fine," Jade said. "I wish you would re-read the journals and report back."

"As you wish," Toby said, a half-smile formed from quivering lips before he disappeared in a puff of smoke.

Malarchy sighed. "I wish you would wait and think things through. I have a feeling there is more to the wishes than we know. Using all three could be dangerous."

"Your father is correct," Gavin added. "There is something not quite right about that little guy."

"Are you sure you aren't upset he insinuated that your kind are born from the belly of true beasts?" Sarah asked. "Perhaps you are more animal than you care to admit."

"Prejudice comes in many forms - some from ignorance and lack of proper education; some from fear of things that are different; and some from a bad experience," Gavin said.

"Sarah," Malarchy started, "what happened to your family was an atrocity, but you can't hold all vampires responsible for the deeds of a handful."

"Letting go of the anger is the road to healing," Simon interrupted. He looked around at the crowd of blank stares. "What?" He held up a pocket book titled *Life After Evil: A Guide to Rehabilitation*. "It's in my manual."

Krissy covered the smirk forming on her face with her hand, but couldn't quite control the laugh. It wasn't for lack of trying and in the end came out as more of a snort than anything else. A swift back hand across her shoulder quickly changed the sound to an *ow*.

"Hey!" Krissy yelled.

Jessica's lips pressed together tightly and her eyes bulged. "Don't discourage him from trying to change," she whispered, her lips moving as little as possible.

Gavin let out his frustrations in a growl. "I think we are getting sidetracked from the real issues. Perhaps we could take a seat around the fire and try to figure out what exactly is going on."

"That sounds like an excellent idea," Naomi said. "We have some information that you may find interesting." She brushed her lips against the cheeks of both Russ and Gavin. A self-confident smile crossed her slightly parted lips as she glanced over at Jade.

"Welcome back," Gavin said. "I take it your travels of this area proved worthy of your time."

"Yes," she answered, placing the long red nail of her middle finger between her teeth - a chuckle escaped from behind.

Chapter Ten

The four vamprite made themselves comfortable while they listened to Malarchy explain the events that had occurred back in Pewterclaw. Other than a few eyerolls from Naomi, the time passed by without incident.

"Well," Gavin said, inhaling and exhaling quickly, "sounds like whatever is going on here is affecting the rest of the main world as well."

"I wouldn't say the rest of the main world," Naomi interrupted. "More like the world that revolves around our precious Jade." Her lips puffed out into a pout then mutated into an O shape. She covered her mouth with her hand. "Maybe she is the Chosen One."

"What?!" Jade screamed.

"Relax," Gavin said, "she's joking."

"Nope," Naomi insisted. "I think it was when Gavin tossed your picture into whoever is behind the rocks." A smile remained plastered to her face, exposing the tips of two sharp teeth. Her tongue brushed against one of the jagged points leaving a line of bright red behind which she applied like lipstick.

Jade's expression morphed from unreadable to disbelief. "You did what?!" she screamed. "If you wanted to be rid of me, you need only ask."

"It wasn't like that," Gavin pleaded, side-eyeing Naomi with a look meant to frighten. "I swear I didn't do that."

"So my daughter's picture is where?" Malarchy asked, his hands locked behind his back.

"It's ... in the cave," Gavin said, sighing. "But I didn't throw it in. It was in my back pocket when I tried to squeeze through to see what was on the other side of the wall. The space wasn't big enough." He turned around and pointed to the missing pocket. "The picture fell in when my pants ripped."

Naomi chuckled. "And now sweet Jade is the Chosen One. He'll be coming for you. You are meant to bear him a child."

That's enough!" Gavin yelled, grabbing Naomi's arm.

"Ow!" she cried, pulling away from him.

72

"What's wrong with your arm?" Gavin asked, the two lines between his eyes pressing in as if trying to join into one.

"That's none of your concern," Naomi scowled.

"I could feel how thick the bandage is you are wearing," Gavin replied. "As part of my team if you are hurt badly, I need to know."

"It's just a scratch," Naomi snapped back. "Maybe a bug bite."

"A bug bite?" Russ questioned. "What bug can penetrate the skin of a vamprite? If you found one, we should study it and warn our people."

"I don't know. I woke up with it," Naomi said. "It'll be gone in a day or two. I think you have more pressing matters to attend to." Her head nodded in Jade's direction. "Don't you want to know what we found out so that you can try to save your darling?"

"I, for one, would like to know," Simon said. "The suspense is killing me."

"Take a seat and hang on," Naomi howled. "This story is going to scare your goosebumps."

"Don't be so dramatic," Delphine scoffed. "From what we can piece together from all the different accounts, sometime ago - no one seems to know exactly when - there were two supreme beings. One, named Mornyx, could only survive in the dark. The other, Raward, had free reign during the day and walked easily after dark as well. Of course, Raward, being more visible, was admired by all.

Mornyx, while equal in power and abilities was, for lack of a better term, neglected."

"This is the part that could read like a good novel written by a master of horror," Naomi interrupted. Light from the fire cast shadows on her face, intensifying the degree of ferocity found in the uneven upward curl of her lips.

"It does," Delphine agreed. "Over time, Mornyx developed several emotions that proved difficult to control. Rather than letting them out, they were kept bottled up until they took on a life of their own - becoming a personal army of sorts."

"Mornyx controlled them; they controlled other life forms," Naomi said, springing forward into a squatting position beside the raging flames of the campfire. "In essence, whoever the emotions took over became a puppet - like in your dreams. Of course, Raward was completely oblivious until it was almost too late."

"Mornyx needed more power," Delphine added.

Simon nodded. "In a world where visibility is everything, one might argue that the darkness is nothing. Is a God who rules nothing really a God?"

"Why doesn't it surprise me you would understand that logic?" Gavin asked.

"The same theory can be just as easily applied to a King," he answered. "It is the basis of my father's struggle throughout the years. It took him over and consumed him. Having time to contemplate his fate made his resolve stronger. If this Mornyx has been bottled up for a long time, madness has already set in."

"Yes!" Naomi squealed. "That's exactly what happened back then as well. To make the darkness something, meant taking away the light. That is what Mornyx set out to do, but his power simply wasn't enough. According to folklore, the first attempt failed - the end result was the very first solar eclipse. Raward was able to counter the spell, returning the sun to full brightness in the sky. The mesh of power, however left a permanent damage."

"Periodic solar eclipses still occur," Sarah said, her fingers typing on a laptop with incredible speed.

"The only way to gain power one doesn't have is to combine abilities with another. For what Mornyx planned, only a child with the same bloodline would be effective." Naomi fell backwards into a cross-legged sitting position. "A mate was chosen. The army of emotions was set loose. Their mission was simple - overtake persons close to the selected one. Not only did it help push the mate to Mornyx, but it also increased the hold of darkness on the world. Raward, however, was ready. A struggle ensued that lasted through seasons."

"Are you explaining why we have daylight savings time without science?" Sarah asked.

"Amazing, isn't it?" Naomi replied. "In the end, Raward was victorious, sealing Mornyx in a tomb of stone - balance was restored."

"If I understand this correctly, you are saying we are facing the possible outbreak of a magically suped-up Cornelius," Malarchy interjected.

"Not necessarily suped-up," Simon said. "What the non-magic of this world consider god-like is simply considered talented to us. Had my father been successful, he might have been considered a God - an evil God, but a God nonetheless. Need I remind you that Willow has the power to bring forth and create new life and she is not a God."

"Of course," Malarchy said, rubbing his chin. "I suppose the tremors that came with Atlantis trying to surface created the original breach."

"That would make some sense," Jessica interrupted. "The magic being used was meant to break a sealed barrier. It could very easily effect other spells and seals."

"Now we know how," Krissy said. "We need to know who."

"I think the who is clear," Sarah said. "The dreams; the lost picture; the book; the strange little man with a secret agenda - it all points to Jade."

"We don't know that for sure," Gavin stated.

"Yeah," Simon said, smacking his lips, "we pretty much do. What we don't know is who is behind the dreams and our lucky leprechaun. While I am leaning towards Mornyx, there is also the possibility Raward is lurking about. The tale didn't seem to mention what happened to the God of Light."

"From what we can gather," Delphine offered, "Raward decided, after sealing away Mornyx, that some levels of power are not meant to exist in this world. It is believed Raward is on an alternate plane, having been self-exiled."

"That sounds familiar," Jessica said, nudging Simon with her elbow.

Simon chuckled. "It would explain the form of dream Jade is having."

"I suggest we set up more tents." Russ said, yawning. "We'll all think better in the morning after some sleep."

"Agreed," Malarchy replied. "I'd like to take a look at the cave, if you don't mind. To ease my mind - I don't want any emotions attacking us."

"Speaking of which," Sarah said. "Do we know which emotions we are dealing with?"

"There is actually a terunji tale about them," Delphine explained. "Gluttony; sloth; envy; greed; wrath; lust; and pride - I believe they have been referred to as deadly sins."

"I believe you are correct," Sarah said, peering over the top of her glasses. "It's a very famous tale. I'll compile a summary for everyone."

"Good," Malarchy said, heading towards the rocky opening - Jade by his side. They stopped at the mouth of the cave. A chill that felt like a scream engulfed them. The darkness beckoned them to move forward.

Jade pushed one foot forward - a few loose pebbles beneath her feet scattered as if frightened by her movement. Malarchy's arm jutted out in front of her, stopping her from moving any further forward.

"No." The word floated off his lips no louder than a whisper but as stern as if he were yelling. "It isn't safe." He looked up at a sky of grey clouds covering the minimal light the moon provided. "We will explore further in the daylight."

"Ow!" Jade exclaimed.

"What's wrong?" her father asked.

"It's nothing," Jade replied. "I think Shelby pecked me." She glanced down at the picture on her arm. "Probably means it's time to move."

"Indeed," Malarchy agreed. "But I have to wonder why the avian guardian didn't simply speak to you."

"I'm not sure," Jade answered. "I don't think I have completely adapted to the connection yet." She rubbed her side. The pain that had become her constant companion over the past few weeks was returning. A pain she wasn't ready to tell anyone else about - at least not yet. "I'm a little tired. I think I should turn in." Her lips brushed against her father's cheek.

"A good plan," Gavin interrupted. "I don't want you anywhere near that cave." His arm intertwined with hers, directing her back towards the camp. He stopped in front of a tent and pointed towards the door. "This is your place. I'm right next door if you need me."

A silence as dark as the night formed between them. The few moments they stood still seemed like an eternity.

"Good night," Jade offered, not able or willing to keep the awkwardness alive. She smiled, ducking her head to enter the tent.

Chapter Eleven

There had been no dreams during the night. There was something in the atmosphere - something Jade couldn't quite put her finger on that was strangling the images before they could form.

"You look perplexed," Simon noted. "Is it because you didn't have your nightmare?"

"How did you know?"

Simon chuckled. "I am a dreamwalker. Last night, something or someone stole all of our dreams. Someone doesn't want us to find answers. Whoever it is doesn't seem to distinguish between normal dreams and the ones you have been having."

"That only leads to more questions," Jade replied.

"The problem is, we don't know if someone is trying to stop us from aiding in the escape of Mornyx or if Mornyx is using us for escape," Malarchy interrupted. "And good morning."

"Whether we like it or not," Simon said, "answers are in that cave. We need a closer look at that dial. The pictures may hold some clues."

"Are you volunteering?" Gavin asked, emerging from his tent. "I have no problem letting you risk your life if you want to."

Simon laughed. "I'm starting to see what my brother liked about the lot of you - you're always joking. It's refreshing."

Malarchy sighed. "The game is the same, but the names have changed." He turned his attention to his daughter. "Perhaps Shelby could take a look around. We could use an aerial view."

"And perhaps you could charter a plane and look yourselves," Shelby snapped, appearing on Jade's shoulder. Her wings spread to their full extent, lifting her into flight.

"She isn't feeling herself," Lasel offered. "This is a hard transition for everyone involved. Jade needs to put a little more effort into our relationship for it to work. A keeper needs to be as willing as her guardian counterparts. There is a necessary bonding - a trust that seems to be lacking."

"Sorry," Jade muttered, kicking the dirt with her shoe.

"Yes," Lasel replied, "we'll talk later. Give Shelby some time - she'll be back. I'll take the flight over the area for you." His wings spread. With a flap he soared upwards vanishing behind the fluffy white clouds.

"I'm not sure I can be like Willow," Jade admitted.

"No one expects you to," Krissy offered. "You need to stop worrying about what you can't be and concentrate on who you are and what you can do."

"I agree," Simon offered. "For whatever reason, you have been chosen. Whether that choice was made by Mornyx or someone else, there is belief you are strong enough to handle any task. You need to answer the call."

Jade's head stayed down, the weight of stares looming over her - demanding an audience. The urge to run; to hide; to escape, encompassed her, strangling her. A whistling noise accompanied a lump rising in her throat. The fast-paced pulsing of blood through her veins matched the sound of her racing heart rate - thumping to a dull ache in her temples. In the background there were concerned voices, but the words meant little. There was no possibility of answering - no words would form.

"She's having a panic attack!" Sarah exclaimed. "Give her air."

A panic attack, she thought. *So that's what this is.* She gasped, sucking in as much air with each breathe as possible. *It's impossible! I can never be strong enough to fight a God.*

Body parts moved without consent. The people she cared about - friends - family, they were trying to help her. Lying down, her father's face came into her line of sight. There, in his eyes, she could see his love for her. The surroundings changed. He'd used this technique before. Whenever she was frightened as a child, he brought her to a place where she could relax, at least enough to fall asleep and forget. She closed her eyes and listened to his voice.

"You're not alone," He said. "Draw strength from your friends - draw strength from me. Whatever your role in this is, we are in it together."

Chapter Twelve

Gavin rubbed his jaw between his thumb and finger. "Thoughts?" he asked.

"Shouldn't we wait for someone to secure the structure of the cave?" Russ asked.

Malarchy's hands brushed against the side of the entrance to the cave. Tiny pebbles and dirt scattered down following his movements. "Not when my daughter is involved," he said, the tone of his voice daring challenge. "If there is even the slightest chance that cave holds the answer, we are going in. Besides, I don't think we will have the luxury of being alone for much longer. This type of magical activity is bound to catch someone else's attention, even with illusions."

"You mean the Department of Secrecy?" Gavin asked.

"There are individuals far worse than Kasper out there, but yes," The mayor answered. "Kasper would make for a sticky situation, to say the least. I don't have to remind you of his feelings about the vamprite. The Organization was more on my radar - as are the elves. Both groups have shown an interest in anything that has power."

"I thought the elves helped you in the past," Russ said, rubbing his neck.

"Indeed," Malarchy replied, returning his attention to the gaping mouth of the cave. "Or, one could argue, they helped us to help themselves. Trust is not something we can afford to give easily. Either way, I'd prefer if Jade didn't become the subject of a power struggle."

Gavin glanced back towards the camp. "I don't suppose we have anyone proficient with a wand, do we?"

Simon chuckled. "Well," he said, pulling a black wand with a white tip out from his pocket, "I might fill that order."

Russ howled. "Are you going to pull a rabbit out from a hat next?"

"Why, are you hungry?" Simon snapped back.

"Perhaps," Malarchy bellowed, "we could focus on the task at hand. Take a look at yourselves. We four are lined up in front of this entrance way - arguing like cowards."

Simon took a few steps backwards, tilting his head from one side to the other. "I see what you mean. We look like food waiting to be devoured. I don't suppose anyone else noticed that the entrance looks like an open mouth." He stepped past the others and reached up to touch one of the stalactite.

"Was that there before?" Russ asked.

"No," Gavin said. "That is definitely new. The shifting and falling rocks must have formed that particular shape."

"Peculiar, isn't it," Simon replied. "Well, let's see what else is in store for us then." A grey glow, similar to smoke, escaped from the tip of his wand. He side-eyed the vamprite, his lips curled up at the edges - daring them to make a move. "Don't worry. I have no intentions of letting myself be buried in stone. As long as we are together you are completely safe."

"How far in do we have to go?" Malarchy asked. A flashlight gripped tightly in his hand cast enough light for the group to see, but also left shadows in places leaving the perfect amount of doubt as to whether or not the four were alone.

"Just up ahead," Gavin replied. "We should see the crevice soon - there!" He pointed to a dim orange glow radiating from a crooked gap. "The size hasn't changed."

Malarchy shone the light over top at the dial, examining each of the crude depictions. The large hand still pointed to one that resembled a dog.

"At least we learnt something," Simon said. "Whoever made that wasn't an artist. Looks like: a dog; a snake, a pig, a peacock; a bear; a goat; and a frog."

"So we are looking for animals?" Russ asked.

"I don't think this is literal," Malarchy explained. "More likely they are symbols - a type of logo. One most likely corresponds to each of the emotions Mornyx gave life to. I expect they have to be completed in sequence."

"So you think the first is complete? Someone has already been infected?" Gavin asked.

"I think the first is underway. If I am correct, the dial will remain in that spot until after whatever the plan is, is completed. Then it will move to the next emotion." Malarchy answered. "I am more interested in the second dial. The speed at which it is moving is too fast to see if there are any meanings."

"Then this has been a waste of time," Russ said. "We don't know any more now than we did before we came in."

"On the contrary," Malarchy said. "We now know an order in which people will be targeted. All we need to do is place the symbol with a name..."

"And figure out who the target it is," Gavin interrupted

"Then figure out how to stop someone from being overtaken. If we take into account the message Tobias wrote in that book of yours, we can assume we are trying to stop feelings - powerful feelings. Even if we figure out the who, how do we stop them from being angry or jealous?"

"That is an excellent question," Malarchy said, shining his light towards a downpour of rocks and dirt. "One I think we should try to answer in a different location."

"Don't trust me?" Simon asked. "I haven't let any dirt mess up your clothes yet."

"Yet being the word that concerns me," Malarchy admitted.

"I'd prefer not to leave Jade alone for too long as well," Gavin declared.

"Agreed," Malarchy said.

Chapter Thirteen

"What an odd time to sleep," Tobias said.

Jade's eyes crossed, trying to focus on the little man standing in front of her nose. "What are you doing?!" she asked. The force of her breath toppled the leprechaun backwards. She extended her hand to stop his tumble.

"That was unexpected. A little more careful in the future," he said.

"You're the one who stood in front of my face while I was sleeping," Jade barked back.

"And you could use a breath mint," Toby snickered, waving a hand in front of his large snout.

Jade gasped. Both her hands covered her mouth. "Is it that bad?" she muttered.

"I wouldn't go kissing that vampire boyfriend of yours," Tobias jested.

"We aren't that serious," Jade replied, dropping him onto a pillow.

"Oh," Toby said, "Trouble in love? Perhaps I could..."

"Absolutely not!" Jade exclaimed.

"I didn't even finish my sentence," Toby complained. "How do you know what I was going to say?"

"It doesn't matter," Jade explained. "I don't want you involved in my love life in any way. Do you understand?"

Tobias stumbled backwards from the force of her finger against his midsection. "Alright," he conceded, waiving his hands back and forth. "No need for violence." He turned his back to her, his arms crossed - hands tucked in.

Jade chuckled at the thought of her finger being able to be violent. "I'm sorry," she said, still chuckling. "I didn't mean to be quite so forceful."

"You didn't think is right," Tobias said. "That's the problem - you aren't thinking."

"What do you mean by that?!" Jade demanded.

"Don't get in a huff, lassie," Toby answered. "It's just you aren't looking at the bigger picture. I have always been a bit of an empath. I can feel your self-doubt." He shoved his hand into his pocket and pulled out a tiny pipe. "Don't worry," he said, puffing out a few times. "It isn't tobacco. It's a special blend only we leprechauns have. It isn't dangerous to anything, including the environment, but still gives the pleasure and taste of a real smoke." The pipe dangled out of the corner of his mouth as he spoke. Every so often his lips tightened allowing him to inhale deeply following which grey smoke escaped through any gap it could find, no matter how small.

Jade coughed. She waved her hand in front of her face to clear the air. "It may not be harmful, but it still stinks," she replied, the edges of her lips curling down like an old-fashioned moustache. "If you want to use your pipe, it should be outside." She opened the flaps and followed the tiny man out.

"Looks who's back," Simon said. "Our lucky leprechaun has returned to join the party. Did you find the publication you were looking for?"

"I," Tobias said, tapping one foot with his hands planted firmly on his hips, "am not your lucky leprechaun. You may refer to me as Tobias Shemus William Murtogh O'Sullivan, the 93rd."

"I thought you dropped the ninety-third," Simon mused.

"I added it back in," Toby replied. "As for the publications, I did indeed find what I was looking for."

"And?!" Simon yelled.

"And," Tobias said, pausing just long enough to achieve maximum irritation, "I can confirm the creature of the night in your stories was the first vampire in existence. A vampire whose blood contained a mutation gene. Followers, as few as there may have been, who drank the blood became carriers. It was the next generation that began to show signs of being affected. Through years of evolution we ended up with the vamprite."

"I don't suppose your records have any information on how to dispose of it, do they?" Malarchy asked.

"And this is your great liaison," Naomi hissed. "A full supporter of vampire rights - ready to kill our ancestor without question. No judge - no jury - only condemnation."

"There's a monster in there," Simon retorted. "We may only have one shot. I think the stories are clear..."

"Clear?" Naomi yelled, her eyes dancing like a wild animal engaged in a primal fight. "Are the terunji tales about us ... clear? Again our kind is persecuted without proof. Our ancestor deserves the right to exist. The right to..."

"Not when it comes to my daughter!" Malarchy bellowed. His voice lowered to almost a whisper, "I'm sorry. I will not put her in harm's way."

Gavin's gaze turned to the mayor. The corners of his lips curled slightly up in defiance. "You would kill the missing link to the vamprite because of a terunji tale and a few dreams? I thought more of you, Malarchy."

"You would risk my daughter to find out if what a leprechaun says is true?" Malarchy retorted, sweat on his brow left to drip down his reddening face. "I thought more of you, Gavin."

"Perhaps," Jade interrupted, "what happens to me is insignificant." She had said it. What everyone was thinking. What she was thinking. A tear streamed down her cheek, meeting up with a droplet of sweat. A ringing in her ears sounded like low laughter. She glanced at each of her shoulders, but Toby was nowhere to be found. The firm grasp of a hand on her arm from behind coupled with the racing of her own heartbeat was too much to bare. She needed to get away - to run away - to be free from everything that was happening and everyone around her. This wasn't the sort of thing she was ready for. Willow was the strong one - not her.

"Wait!" Gavin yelled.

Jade stopped in her tracks. "What?" she answered.

"Take your hands off my daughter," Malarchy demanded, pushing Gavin to the ground.

"It doesn't have to be like this!" Gavin cried.

"Yes, it does!" Jade screamed, turning to face the two most important men in her life. "I thought I could count on you." She swallowed back the saliva pooling in her mouth to try to calm her stomach. Throwing up wasn't going to help.

"Do you know what you are asking?" Gavin questioned.

"I'm asking you to believe me," Jade screamed back. "My dreams aren't about a great leader coming to save your people - they are nightmares born from the emotions of a beast." Her arms fell to her sides, limp. "In the end, it doesn't matter. This isn't something we can battle. We can't stop someone from being angry or jealous. Even if we could, we don't know who, when or where."

"We'll figure it out," Malarchy responded.

"How?!" Jade screamed. "We don't know where to begin."

"We start with what we do know," Malarchy answered, placing his arms around his daughter. "We know why. We know the people affected will be close to the Chosen One. These puppets have been infected with negative emotions and are meant to somehow drive you closer to Morynx."

Gavin brushed the dirt from his pants. "I'm sorry," he said, his head hanging down. "I need some time to think." He walked away without looking at a soul.

Laughter followed his steps. This time, it was clear where it came from. Naomi's smile couldn't have become larger. "Trouble in paradise?" she cackled. "I think I'll go pick up the pieces."

There was nothing to do except watch her skip away as if she were playing a childhood game of some sort.

"I can't do this," Jade cried in her father's arms. "I'm not strong enough."

"You are stronger than you know," Malarchy responded, his lips gently brushing a kiss on his daughter's forehead. "Believe in yourself, the way I believe in you."

Chapter Fourteen

The last time Jade had been in the command centre had been to say goodbye to Willow and William. Things were different now. Zsiga sat in the seat that had always represented leadership. She closed her eyes and envisioned everyone who was missing. A smile graced her lips from the memories, but that was all they were now - memories. She shook her head. It was time - time to move on and accept that what once was, wasn't anymore.

"Fascinating," Miss Kelly said, slapping Cornost before he could kiss her hand. "If what you say is true, this Mornyx and Raward are from before our arrival."

"How can that be?" Sarah asked. "I thought you were here at the beginning of existence."

"Goodness no," Miss Kelly replied. "There was life here before we arrived that none of us know anything about. Unfortunately, we weren't interested in events of the past - we were looking towards our own future. It does, however, shed some light on eclipses. I could never figure out why I had no control over them. This makes some sense." She swatted Cornost again, this time for no apparent reason.

"Perhaps your play time would be better served outside this meeting," Malarchy snapped.

"I agree wholeheartedly, however, I am stuck with him until he finds his true love. The particular spell the fates used is unbreakable by anything else. Of course, should the spell break, we will be faced with the evil king who almost destroyed us all. I don't think any of us want that."

"Yes," Malarchy agreed. "I see your point."

"Getting back to the issue at hand," Zsiga said, clearing his throat, "how do we find these puppets? They could be anyone."

"No," Malarchy said. "They have to be someone that has a connection to the Chosen One or at least be in a position to impact her life."

"Are you sure it's Jade?" Miss Kelly asked. "How do you know for certain?"

"I suppose we don't - at least not one hundred percent," Malarchy replied. "But the signs aren't pointing towards anyone else. Only Jade is having the dreams. Then there is the matter of the leprechaun and his use of the Portal Prophecies book."

"Yes," Miss Kelly said, rubbing the spot where a whisker was growing from her chin. "I suppose that does point towards the girl."

"I am here," Jade muttered, without being acknowledged.

"I can't be the only one thinking this leprechaun has his own agenda," Simon said. "Can we really afford to trust him?"

"I heard that," Tobias snarled, appearing on Jade's shoulder. "Whether you trust me or not, I am bound to the Miss until all three wishes have been made."

"This is hopeless," Jade cried, throwing her head into her hands. "How can we ever figure out who the puppets are in time?"

"Well," Miss Kelly answered. "There would have to be signs. Using that strong of a magic on an individual always leaves a mark. Cornost, remove your shirt, please." She ran her fingers over his chest. "As blind as I am, I don't need to use my third eye to know the point of entry of the fates' arrows left a scar. Knowing those three, it probably is little hearts."

"Indeed," Malarchy said, his eyebrows bunched and top lip raised at the sight. "An explanation would have sufficed. The visual we could have done without."

"Yes, well, the fates hate it when no one notices the little details they put into their work and I am blind," Miss Kelly said, adding an unnerving laugh at the end. "The point is, if you identify one mark, you'll know what to look for."

"That does give us something to look for," Sarah said. "Even if it is rather vague."

"Perhaps," Simon said, "if I may suggest, we start in this room. Eliminate the chance that any of us are already infected by these emotions."

"Emotions," Jade repeated. "Love is an emotion."

"Yes, dear," Malarchy replied.

"Love is represented by hearts at the entry point," Jade said, the wooden floor creaking in the same places with each pass she made. "On the dials were pictures of animals - one for each emotion. Those could be what we are looking for."

"It's a longshot," Jessica said.

"It's the best we have," Malarchy added. "Micca can handle medical examinations of all camp members."

"What about your vampire friends?" Simon asked.

"I doubt they will agree to an examination," Jade answered. "They won't be helping us this time." Her gaze never left the twiddling of her own thumbs.

"You're not alone, Jade," Krissy said. "We are here to help you."

The words soothed the butterflies in Jade's stomach. It was nice to know she had friends who would back her up if she needed it. There was, however, no way to completely silence the nagging inside herself. She was picked for this fight for a reason. If there was one thing she learnt from Willow, there are some things that people need to do for themselves - some things that people can't rely on friends and family for. It was time for her to step up and answer the call.

Author's message

I hope you enjoyed reading *Answering the Call* as much as I did writing it. Watch for new books in this series.

Envy

Pride

Gluttony

Lust

Wrath

Greed

Sloth

Other titles coming soon from C.A. King

Shattering the Effect of Time

Join the Shinning brothers, Jessie, Dezi and Pete as they set out on a quest to save their younger sister. No magic known to them or their friends has ever been able to reverse the grip of time. A few legends, however, exist mentioning ancient items that may hold the key to do exactly that.

This brand new series will take you on a search for the fountain of youth and mermaids; a quest for the Holy Grail; a trip to visit Daryl the mountain guru, in the hunt for the Cinamani Stone; on a search for ambrosia, the food of the gods; and other adventures.

Tomoiya's Story: Collecting Tears

Graduation as co-valedictorian of her high school class, along with her best friend Moira, was icing on the cake. There was no doubt, Tomoiya, a princess of a wealthy kingdom, was born for greatness. She had everything: intelligence; good looks; popularity; and a secret. Not even her closest friends were allowed to know she was a vampire.

One night was all it took to change everything. When celebrations turned deadly, Tomoiya was forced to come face-to-face with the realization she wasn't the only one amongst her peers with something to hide.

Tomoiya's stuck asking the question if she can ever trust anyone again and there is nobody to answer except herself.

Tomoiya's Story: Stalked

Woden's war did more than anyone could imagine. When rival races wage war against each other, Tomoiya's life is again at risk. Is there anywhere safe for a golden vampiric princess?

The Portal Prophecies

These great titles in C.A. King's The Portal Prophecies series are available now at most online book retailers:

A Keeper's Destiny

A Halloween's Curse

Frost Bitten

Sleeping Sands

Deadly Perceptions

Finding Balance

The prophecies are the key to their survival. Can they solve them in time?